W9-AMR-629

The Full Moon

Read all the books in
The Faeries' Promise series:

Silence and Stone
Following Magic
Wishes and Wings

The Faeries' Promise
The Full Moon

BY KATHLEEN DUEY

Illustrated by
SANDARA TANG

Aladdin
New York London Toronto Sydney

With love and thanks to Ellen Krieger,
my editor and friend, for publishing my first book
and so many more

This book is a work of fiction. Any references to historical events, real people, or real locales are used fictitiously. Other names, characters, places, and incidents are the product of the author's imagination, and any resemblance to actual events or locales or persons, living or dead, is entirely coincidental.

ALADDIN

An imprint of Simon & Schuster Children's Publishing Division
1230 Avenue of the Americas, New York, NY 10020
First Aladdin hardcover edition July 2011
Text copyright © 2011 by Kathleen Duey
Illustrations copyright © 2011 by Sandara Tang
All rights reserved, including the right of reproduction in whole or in part in any form.
ALADDIN is a trademark of Simon & Schuster, Inc., and related logo
is a registered trademark of Simon & Schuster, Inc.
Available in Aladdin hardcover and paperback editions.
For information about special discounts for bulk purchases, please contact Simon & Schuster Special
Sales at 1-866-506-1949 or business@simonandschuster.com.
The Simon & Schuster Speakers Bureau can bring authors to your live event. For more information
or to book an event contact the Simon & Schuster Speakers Bureau at 1-866-248-3049 or visit our
website at www.simonspeakers.com.
Designed by Lisa Vega
The text of this book was set in Adobe Garamond.
The illustrations for this book were rendered digitally.
Manufactured in the United States of America 0611 FFG
2 4 6 8 10 9 7 5 3 1
Library of Congress Cataloging-in-Publication Data
Duey, Kathleen.
The full moon / by Kathleen Duey ; illustrated by Sandara Tang. — 1st Aladdin hardcover ed.
p. cm. — (The faeries' promise ; [#4])
Summary: After many trials and much adversity, the faeries have returned to their meadow home, but
Lord Dunraven vows that they must not remain.
ISBN 978-1-4169-8462-7 (hardcover)
[1. Fairies—Fiction. 2. Magic—Fiction.] I. Tang, Sandara, ill. II. Title.
PZ7.D8694Fu 2011
[Fic]—dc22
2010019165
ISBN 978-1-4424-1300-9 (eBook)

Alida is a faerie princess and Gavin is a human boy. Alida spent many years locked in a castle tower before Gavin helped her escape. They are friends, even though old Lord Dunraven's law forbids friendship between faeries and humans. That same law forced Alida's family to live in hiding, far from their home in the forest near the village of Ash Grove. But they have come back to the meadow where faeries lived for a thousand years before the law. And they intend to stay there.

Chapter

1

Summer was gone.

Nights were getting chilly.

One morning Alida could see her breath as she sat up in the nest she shared with her sister. Terra was already awake.

Alida stretched and tucked her wings under her shawl.

Then she followed Terra downward through the branches of the massive old oak tree. The edges of the leaves were turning brown.

The sun was barely up, but the meadow was already full of faeries.

No one was flying. They were all walking, their

1

wings hidden beneath cloaks and capes and shawls.

Every day Alida's mother made sure there were faeries perched high in the trees, watching the forest and listening for the sound of hoofbeats. No one knew when Lord Dunraven's guards might come looking for them again.

Near the middle of the meadow, Alida waved at her sister and Terra waved back.

Then they both hurried to begin their work. Today Alida would help weave sturdy floor mats from river grass.

There was a lot to do before winter closed in. The day before, she had helped her aunt Lily sort through all their blankets. Some had been torn on the journey home. Aunt Lily had taught her a simple mending magic. It had been hard at first, but Alida had practiced it until she could help repair the old blankets.

They would need many new blankets and warmer clothes before winter came. The weavers were doing everything they could to get their looms up and working.

Most of the faeries were headed toward a wide, tangled circle of berry bushes and sapling trees. Any human coming into the meadow would think the bushes were part of the forest. That was exactly what the faeries wanted them to think.

But they weren't.

Alida had searched for seedlings in the woods. Everyone had. They replanted them here, in huge, crooked circles.

A slender mulberry tree Alida had carried home was twice as tall already. The young blackberries, blueberries, wild pear trees, and woods' roses had all grown incredibly fast too.

Alida's mother said there was a thousand years worth of magic in the soil. Her sister Lily said it was even older than that.

Whatever it was, the uneven circle of trees and bushes was tall enough to hide the weavers' and cheese makers' houses the faeries had built—and their storage sheds.

They had planted a second circle of jumbled trees and bushes at the other end of the meadow. That one hid a pasture for their cows and goats.

Alida looked at the faeries around her. Almost no one was talking. No one was smiling or singing.

The faerie flutes and harps were packed away. No one dared to play music in the evenings now.

Everyone was worried. They were always ready to run.

Everyone knew exactly what to do.

If Lord Dunraven's guards came, the faeries would race to the tall oak tree on the edge of the clearing. They would stand close together so Alida's mother could use her new magic to make them invisible.

It had worked twice.

Both times, when the guards couldn't see anyone, they had left.

Alida sighed. Her mother had taught her the magic too, just in case. Every night before she went to sleep she recited the odd, ancient words. She practiced gathering her own magic and reciting the names of all the faeries, too.

Alida knew the guards would probably come again, sooner or later.

And when they did, it would be her fault. She was the one who had helped the humans. She was the one they had seen.

Walking to the creek to gather a stack of tall, strong grass, Alida made herself stop worrying long enough to concentrate on the new magic she was experimenting with. It wasn't big magic.

It was small magic—the safest kind.

First she used the usual cutting magic her father had taught her and watched a wide swath of the tough, wiry grass fall neatly on the ground.

Then she tried to mend it.

About half of the grass jerked upright and balanced on its stems, but then it fell over again.

She tried a second time, then a third.

The fourth time, some of the grass repaired itself, the stems as strong as if she had never cut them at all. Alida smiled, gathered up the rest, and walked back to the clearing.

All morning she helped two of her sister's friends and a few elder faeries weave mats for the floor of the weavers' house.

As usual, most of the elders acted like she wasn't there.

Kary and Cinder were nice, but Alida could tell they were a little uneasy around her too.

Everyone was.

Alida didn't blame them. It wasn't just because the villagers had seen her and knew the faeries had come home. She was *different*. She had grown up by herself, locked in a castle tower. Her best friend was a human boy and she missed him every day. That was very hard for the other faeries to understand.

Gavin and his grandmother lived in Ruth Oakes's cottage near Ash Grove. It wasn't that far away, but she couldn't go visit him. And he was afraid to visit her.

Lord Dunraven's great-grandfather had made the cruel law long ago. Friendship between faeries and humans was still forbidden. They were not allowed even to *talk* to each other.

Alida's family had tried to obey the law. They moved to a meadow far from this one, in a place where no humans lived. They had stayed there a long, long time until Alida's mother realized the faeries couldn't be happy—or healthy—anywhere but here.

So they had come home, traveling at night, following hidden forest paths. Gavin had helped them move back.

Almost all the faeries had come to like him very much. But they were still afraid to have him come visit.

"Alida?"

She turned at the sound of her mother's voice.

"Have you seen your sister?"

"Terra's helping Aldous and his family," an elder faerie answered before Alida could.

"Thank you, William," Alida's mother called as she turned away, walking fast.

Today, like most days, she was dressed in plain clothes. She would work alongside everyone else.

If Lord Dunraven's guards ever rode into the meadow looking for the queen of the faeries, they wouldn't be able to tell which one she was.

Alida's mother was always busy. Every single argument, every problem, every decision, was her concern.

Almost every decision.

Alida lowered her head so no one could see the worry in her eyes.

When she had decided to help the people in Ash Grove, she had kept it a secret because she didn't want anyone to try to stop her.

Lord Dunraven's guards came to the village every year in big, creaking wagons pulled by tall horses. They always demanded a share of everything the farmers had raised, and hauled the food back to Lord Dunraven's castle.

Lord Dunraven owned the forest.

He owned the towns and the farms.

And this year, he had ordered his guards to take more than usual, even though it meant some of the human families might starve. Alida wasn't sorry she had flown to each farm in the dark of night and used her mother's new magic to make half the harvest invisible.

But half the town had *seen* her when she came back to remove the magic.

After so many years of hiding, she had been the one to ruin everything.

The humans in Ash Grove knew the faeries had come back. If they told Lord Dunraven's guards, there would be terrible trouble.

Alida had no idea how to repair the damage she had done.

She only knew she had to try.

Chapter

2

Three days later, when Alida and Terra's friends finished weaving the mats, her mother asked her to help the cheese makers. They put her to work washing curds.

It was hard, but simple, work.

So while Alida carried heavy buckets of clean water and sloshed the big oaken tubs, she found herself worrying about Lord Dunraven and his guards.

She hoped the people of Ash Grove were glad she had helped them—and grateful enough to keep the faeries' secret. Everyone was hoping the same thing. Her mother thought they would.

But Alida wasn't sure.

Most of the people of Ash Grove were very poor.

If Lord Dunraven offered a reward of silver coins, maybe someone would tell him that the faeries had come home, that they had *seen* one.

That evening at supper, everyone sat at the old wooden tables, eating lily blossom soup and listening.

Alida's father was talking about digging a winter shelter inside the circle of transplanted bushes and trees—just in case.

"The adults can use magic to stay warm," he said. "But some of our families have two or three little ones. That much magic-making is exhausting. And the elders . . ."

"I've made my way through more storms than anyone else here," William interrupted. "And this seems foolish to me. We should be working to store food, not digging holes."

"But if a storm lasts long enough," Alida's father

said, "we could all get exhausted—too weak to work magic of any kind."

Her mother leaned forward. "We are going to make a shelter."

Alida had never heard her sound so stern.

No one argued with her. Not even William.

The next day Alida's father and seven other men started digging inside the first circle of bushes and trees, as far from the weavers' house and the other buildings as they could.

Before long, Alida saw piles of dirt rising out of the hole, lifted by magic.

At supper one evening, her father told everyone he was going to use a new kind of binding magic and thick, straight logs to make the walls incredibly strong.

As he spoke, Alida noticed little cuts and bruises on his hands. Even with magic to help, the work the men were doing was hard.

Every day the hole was deeper and wider. She

asked her father how big the shelter would be, and he told her he hadn't decided yet.

That made Alida wonder.

Maybe he wasn't just concerned about bad weather.

The next day Alida's father had some of the faeries start collecting logs in the forest.

Terra decided to go with Aldous and his family again. Alida knew why.

"I'll help the weavers again today," Alida said one morning as they climbed down the tree.

Terra smiled. "I'm still helping Aldous and his family. I'm getting good at spotting the best logs, and I like walking in the woods all day."

"You like *Aldous,*" Alida said.

Terra's cheeks turned a deep shade of pink as she perched on the lowest branch. "I do. But the work is important. Father says he needs hundreds of logs to brace the walls."

Alida blinked. *Hundreds?* "I don't remember having a winter shelter before. Did we?"

Terra shook her head. "Not like this one. But we had cottages here for the worst storms—and there were caves at the other place." She jumped to the ground.

Alida followed, then leaned close to whisper. "I think the shelter isn't just for bad weather. I think it's a place to hide when the guards come."

Terra's eyes widened. "That makes sense," she said, then smiled when Aldous shouted and waved from across the meadow.

Alida watched her sister run toward him. Then a high-pitched giggle overhead made her look up. Kary and Cinder were playing. Cinder had slipped, and she was hanging over the edge of their nest, her rose-colored wings spread wide.

Alida heard Cinder's father scolding them, and the giggling stopped. Cinder climbed back into the nest and put on her shawl to hide her wings.

Alida walked faster. She slipped through the berry bushes and started toward the weavers' house. She passed the cheese makers' open door on the way. They were already at work.

Both buildings were sturdy and clever. The faeries had no saws, nails, or hammers. Even small amounts of iron burned their skin. They couldn't use metal tools. That was why they used magic to dig and cut grass.

In the old days, before Dunraven's law, they would have traded a little magic to hire human carpenters to build workhouses and sheds for them. But now they had to make new magic.

After a lot of experimenting, Alida's father had invented magic that cut wood as well as a saw. Her mother had created a binding magic strong enough to use instead of nails.

When Alida went through the weavers' door, she heard a clacking sound. The looms were working!

There were two big rooms, one for the looms and

one for spinning. The faeries used magic for both, so thread was being spun and cloth was being woven on six different looms, with just two faeries tending everything. One of them was Kary's cousin Iris. She was picking through a basket of madder root and stirring a steaming dye pot.

"What needs doing?" Alida asked her.

Iris led her into a smaller room.

Alida ended up sitting on a low wooden stool beside a huge basket of fluffy white balls. Her job was to separate the softest thistledown silk from the stiffer fibers for the spinners. At first it seemed impossible. It got easier, but the morning crawled past.

Late that afternoon, Alida heard the front door open and close. "Where do you want these?" someone called out. No one answered, so Alida went to look.

A young faerie named Emma was carrying an armload of spider boxes. Alida knew that the weavers

fed the spiders and kept them warm in the winter in trade for endless threads of spider silk. But she had never seen them before.

Iris came in to help Emma just as a gray-haired faerie named May carried in more boxes. Neither of them spoke to Alida.

She went back to work, glad spider-feeding wasn't her chore. At least not yet.

As she sat down on her stool, a sudden clattering sound startled her. She stood up again, her heart thudding. May gasped, and the looms stopped clicking.

Alida listened, ready to run to the tall oak tree at the edge of the woods.

Then the sound came again, and she exhaled. It was just a woodpecker on the roof. She sat down and went back to work. Everyone did. But they were all on edge.

Later Alida overheard two of the elders talking about her.

"There will be more trouble," William was telling Aunt Lily and a woman named Girta. "Our princess Alida has a human friend. Her *best* friend, she says." He paused, and when he spoke again, his voice was a little louder. "Why didn't the humans in Ash Grove ever come to thank her if they were truly grateful?"

Alida reached for another ball of thistledown.

She knew why no one had come.

The people of Ash Grove were scared to be seen anywhere near this meadow. They were as afraid of Lord Dunraven's guards as the faeries were.

Alida's father was still working on the shelter when she went to supper. She could hear his voice from down in the wide hole. He sounded tired. Everyone was working so hard.

"Do you think we'll have everything ready before the snow comes?" Terra asked her once they were settled for the night.

Alida looked up at the stars. Then she turned to

face her sister. "Sometimes it seems like no one even wants to talk to me now."

"Everyone's just afraid of the guards coming," Terra said. "They are proud of what you did."

Alida wanted to believe that.

Long after her sister was asleep, she lay awake, hoping it was true.

Chapter

3

The next day several of the elders bade Alida good morning.

It made her smile.

Later she overheard them talking when she was sorting thistledown.

"We have that new binding magic," her aunt Lily was saying. "And they figured out how to cut wood. We don't need the villagers' help. We could build pretty little houses like the ones we had when I was a girl."

Alida kept her eyes on her work.

She wasn't the one to explain to the elders that they couldn't build pretty little houses anymore— unless they could hide them.

There wasn't much room left inside the circle of bushes and trees now.

They had already built the cheese makers' house, the weavers' house, and sheds to store their carts and harnesses. One of the smallest sheds was for their flutes and faerie harps. And beyond all of that, the hole for the shelter was getting bigger every day.

"Are your hands getting sore?"

Alida looked up.

It was Trina, one of Terra's friends. "A little," Alida told her.

Trina smiled and nodded. "The thistledown is stiff. You should do some other kind of work now and then, or they will get worse."

Alida thanked her.

Midmorning, two other girls stopped to talk.

It made Alida happy, until she suddenly wondered if her sister had asked everyone to be nicer to her.

After two more of the weavers made a point of asking how she was doing, Alida was almost sure that *someone* had told everyone to be nicer.

Maybe Terra had said something to their mother.

Most of the faeries would do anything their queen asked them to do.

Upset, Alida threw the next three wads of soft thistledown into the basket.

She missed Gavin. No one had to tell him to be nice to her. He was her friend because he cared about her.

Alida knew that if she flew fast, she could be at Ruth Oakes's house before dark. No. She should fly at night when no one could see her, but then Terra might wake up and worry.

Alida spent the afternoon planning ways to visit Gavin without anyone finding out.

It wouldn't be difficult.

Ruth Oakes and Gavin's grandmother lived outside town.

There were tall trees around the house. She could get up early and fly in the gray light of dawn, then perch up high and wait until he came out to do his chores.

She just wanted to talk to him—to make sure he was all right—then she would fly home, staying low, through the woods.

When the weavers finally stopped work for the day, Alida ran to find her mother.

She explained her plan. "I know I can't stay long," she said. "I would be very careful and—" She stopped because her mother was shaking her head.

"I know you and Gavin are good friends," she said quietly, "but you need to make faerie friends too."

Alida nodded "I will. I am," she said. "But I—"

"Don't go," her mother whispered. "It's just too dangerous right now." She bent to kiss Alida's cheek, then left. Alida watched her cross the meadow, talking to the faeries she passed, solving problems, making decisions, as always.

The following day Alida separated thistledown and listened to the faeries arguing about whether to spin the new thread with half spider silk, or less than half, so the blankets would be warmer—but a little heavier.

Their voices rose and fell.

And now and then, someone walking past stopped to talk about nothing at all. Alida was polite, but now she was sure her mother had asked them to be nicer.

It was embarrassing.

At noon, when the rest of the faeries were eating cheese and dried lily blossoms, she found her mother.

"I would rather do something outside," she said, "and practice some magic. Maybe I could collect logs for the winter shelter?"

Her mother smiled. "With your sister and—"

"No," Alida interrupted. The last thing she wanted was to have her mother talk anyone into being nice to her all day. She forced herself to smile.

"The weavers' house is noisy and full of people all day—I am looking forward to being alone."

Her mother hesitated. For a moment, Alida thought she was going to say no, but she didn't. "Make sure no one sees you," she said. "If the people of Ash Grove think we are foolish, they'll never trust us. And be very careful."

"I will," Alida promised.

"Is your lifting magic strong enough?"

Alida nodded. "I think so."

Her mother smiled. "Everything will get better. You'll see. We have to be patient."

Alida watched her mother walk away, taking long, quick strides. She probably had ten or fifteen things to settle before supper.

Being the queen of the faeries wasn't easy.

Alida started off. She walked around the circle of bushes and trees that hid the pasture full of their cows and goats. On her way, she passed the big egg-shaped stone where she and Terra had learned to fly.

27

None of the young faeries were practicing now; her mother had asked them not to.

At the edge of the meadow, she waved at the two little girl faeries perched in the trees, watching for Dunraven's guards.

Once she was deep in the woods, Alida unknotted her shawl and turned toward the creek.

Beside it, she stopped and looked around, listening.

When she was absolutely sure no one was nearby, she spread her wings and glided across the water, then put her shawl back on.

After days of listening to clattering looms, the silence in the woods was wonderful.

A rabbit ran in front of her, and she stopped to watch it disappear into the grass.

When she came across a deer path, she followed it.

Most of the big logs she saw were rotten, or curved, or too small. When she finally spotted a good one, she gathered her magic.

The heavy log rose upward, but it rocked and swayed, and Alida dropped it. She tried again. The same thing happened. She widened the magic, and that helped a little, but not enough. She finally tried separating the magic, pushing half of it toward each end of the log.

That worked perfectly.

Alida placed the log next to the deer path, then started looking for more.

She found two.

They were both big. She wasn't sure she could lift all three at once.

It was very hard.

She had to try over and over, but she managed it.

Smiling, starting home, she discovered that it was much easier to balance the logs if she wasn't walking through bushes and tall grass. But the path wove back and forth through the woods. Alida struggled to guide the logs around the sharp turns.

As she got better at it, she experimented with

lifting the logs higher, then lowering them so they skimmed the ground.

She was coming around a long curve in the path when she heard someone shout. Startled, she let the magic lapse and all three logs crashed to the ground. She jumped back when the biggest one bounced and rolled.

Then, over the sound of her own quickened breath, Alida heard hoofbeats.

She ran.

Chapter

4

Fear tightened Alida's stomach even after she realized it wasn't twenty or thirty horses. It was only two, or maybe three, and there was no clanking of armor or sword scabbards.

So it wasn't Lord Dunraven's guards.

But she still couldn't let anyone see her.

Peering through the trees, she got a glimpse of a dun-colored horse, then a beautiful white one. Its rider wore a bright red jacket.

The riders were not from Ash Grove. The people in the village were poor. Their clothes were plain and sturdy. Their horses had rough coats.

Alida had seen riders like these once before.

Gavin had told her they were almost certainly nobles, relatives of the lords of the lands.

"James! I'm winning!" It was a girl's voice, high and clear.

There was another shout, a boy this time. Alida couldn't quite hear what he said. Whatever it was, it made the girl laugh.

The horses were getting closer, galloping hard.

The grass was tall, and Alida found a place where she could wriggle into the tangle of bushes. She held her breath and listened.

The riders were racing, having fun, not searching every clump of bushes.

They would go right past her soon, and they would be busy watching the grassy ground in front of them for old stumps and . . .

Alida caught her breath.

Or maybe they were galloping on the deer path? If they were, they would expect it to be clear, not blocked by the heavy logs she had dropped.

Her heart pounding, Alida crawled forward and scrambled to her feet. She was forming the magic in her mind as the hoofbeats got louder.

She lifted the logs, but she was so scared that they slid and shifted. The biggest one fell. She moved the other two off the path, then started over with the big one.

The log was in midair when the white mare came around the wide curve, galloping hard.

Alida jerked backward, and the log fell across the dirt path. Terrified, she sank to her knees in the bushes just as the startled girl tried to rein her mare in.

It was too late. The mare tried to jump the log, but one forehoof ticked the heavy wood and she stumbled.

Alida flinched as the mare squealed and fell, then scrambled to stand up.

The girl was jolted out of her saddle.

Alida gasped and ducked.

She heard the mare trotting away.

"Ellen?" the boy was yelling. "Are you all right?"

There was no answer.

"ELLEN!?" he shouted.

Alida crouched lower. She could hear his horse slowing as he reined it in.

She waited for him to jump to the ground and run toward the girl.

But he didn't.

A moment later Alida heard hoofbeats. This time, they were fading. The boy was riding away to get help.

The girl moaned, soft and low.

After that there was no sound at all except the jingle of the mare's bridle as she grazed.

Alida shivered. She was afraid to come out of her hiding place. But if Ellen was truly hurt, not just shaken, and scared . . .

The near silence of the woods pressed against Alida's skin. She heard the trees rustling when a tiny breeze came up. The startled birds began to sing again.

Alida hoped desperately that the boy didn't have far to ride, that there were other humans close by.

At any moment, she told herself, she would hear riders coming to help.

But the silence went on, broken only by the usual sounds in the woods—woodpeckers in the pines, mice scuttling through the oak leaves.

Alida crawled out into the sunlight and stood up slowly.

She could see the girl lying in the grass beside the path. She was Gavin's age, or a little younger. Her beautiful red silk jacket had been torn. Her eyes were closed, and Alida saw tears on her cheeks.

The panicked mare had tumbled one of the logs, and it had somehow rolled across the girl's right ankle.

Alida moved as far back as she could, so that if the girl opened her eyes, the grass and bushes would hide her. Then she made the lifting magic quickly and pushed it away from herself, toward the log.

She held her breath and lifted it gracefully, quickly, straight upward, then sideways.

The mare jerked her head up to watch the log float past, then went back to grazing as Alida lowered it into the grass, slowly and silently, well away from the path.

Ellen moved a little.

Alida shrank back, so the tall grass was between them.

"James?" Ellen said. "You don't need to hide. I'll make sure my father doesn't blame you."

Alida pressed her lips together.

"James?"

Alida took one step forward.

"Is my mare all right?"

Alida was afraid to answer. She was about to step backward again when Ellen suddenly sat up, letting out a little cry of pain. Then she spoke. "Who— who are you?"

Alida had no idea what to say. She touched the

knot that held her shawl in place and folded her wings even closer against her back.

"Do you live near here?" Ellen was sitting straighter, lifting her chin, stretching up to try and see over the tall grass.

"I think your friend went to get help," Alida said, to keep from answering the question.

Ellen sighed. "He might be too scared to tell anyone."

"*Why?*" The word leapt out of Alida's mouth.

"My name is Ellen Dunraven."

Alida was stunned. She turned away and stared at the trees. Gavin had told her once that Lord Dunraven had no heir, no one to take over the castle when he got old and died. She had thought he meant Lord Dunraven had no children—but she had misunderstood.

He had meant that Lord Dunraven had no *son*.

"I know most of the people in the villages are afraid of my father," Ellen said quietly. "He's very strict."

Strict?

Alida turned and looked into Ellen's eyes.

Her father was more than strict.

He was cruel. He took more and more of the farmers' harvests. He enforced the terrible law that had made faeries leave their home.

But Alida knew that none of that was Ellen's fault. Maybe she didn't even know about it.

Ellen shifted her legs and winced.

She tried to stand up, but she couldn't put any weight on her right foot. She hopped twice, then sat down again, hard. "My father's in Ash Grove with his guards," she whispered. Then she winced and lowered her head.

Alida saw a bump just above Ellen's ankle that shouldn't have been there. She wanted to help, but she was afraid to try. Her mending magic was good enough for holes in blankets, and river grass, not human bones—surely Ellen's father had a healer at his castle.

Or maybe her father would ask Ruth Oakes to help.

Ruth would help anyone she could. She was the kindest person Alida had ever met.

Alida stepped forward. "If I help you get on your mare," she said quietly, "could you ride back to Ash Grove?"

"Yes." Ellen tipped her head. "Are you strong enough?"

Alida nodded.

She walked closer and reached out. Ellen gripped her hands and struggled upright. She managed to stand, balancing awkwardly on one foot. Alida put one arm around Ellen's waist and steadied her.

With Alida holding her, Ellen hopped to a sapling oak tree. She leaned on it for balance, breathing hard. Her eyes were glassy with tears and her lips were pressed together.

Alida knew her mother could almost certainly heal Ellen.

She also knew she couldn't take Ellen back to the meadow, or bring her mother here. This was Lord Dunraven's daughter!

"I'll get your horse," Alida said.

She walked fast and veered off the path and into the trees so Ellen wouldn't notice the shape of her wings beneath her shawl.

Leading the mare back, Alida tried desperately to think of a way to help Ellen without putting her own family in danger.

She couldn't.

Tightening her wings against her back, she tethered the mare to a tree. Then Ellen leaned heavily on her arm, hopping closer to the mare, stopping when it hurt too much.

When Ellen was ready, Alida boosted her from behind.

Ellen cried out, but she got her left foot in the stirrup and then lifted her injured right leg over the mare's back.

She was breathing hard, but she settled herself and thanked Alida.

Alida held the reins for a moment more.

Then she stepped back.

Ellen sighed and took three or four deep breaths. "I wish I lived in a village like you do."

Alida shook her head. "No, you don't. The people of Ash Grove work hard every day and barely have enough—"

"But you have friends," Ellen interrupted. "People aren't afraid of you. You can go where you want to—no one locks you up in your room to keep you safe." Her voice was pinched with pain. "I am alone, almost all the time, in my chamber in the castle."

Alida blinked, remembering how lonely she had been locked in the tower.

Ellen exhaled. "The silence is like a weight sometimes. Our stableman taught me to ride. I am so grateful to him. Being able to gallop in the woods sometimes is the only freedom I have, and—"

The sound of hoofbeats startled them both. This time Alida could hear the metallic sound of the armor that Lord Dunraven's guards wore.

"The guards will be all too glad to blame you for this," Ellen whispered. "Run!"

Alida sprinted into the woods. She hid in the tall grass.

Peeking out, she spotted the riders. James was leading the way; two guards were with him. He *had* gone for help.

Ellen pulled her mare around and rode slowly down the path toward them. She held her right foot out awkwardly, the empty stirrup swinging.

Alida watched the guards rein in and surround Ellen. She spoke with them, then led the way as they all rode off, at a walk.

Alida waited until they were out of sight. Then she waited a little longer before she finally gathered up the logs and started home.

Alida was sure that Ellen hadn't suspected she was a faerie.

But maybe she would later, when she had time to think about it.

Once her bruises began to show, she might remember that the heavy log had fallen across her ankle—and she would know that a human girl couldn't possibly have moved it.

Chapter

5

Alida meant to tell her parents what had happened as soon as she got home.

But as she crossed the meadow, she heard angry voices. She peeked through the tangle of bushes that hid their buildings and saw her mother and father facing a crowd of faeries.

"Climbing the trees makes my knees ache," William complained.

Alida's aunt Lily was frowning too. "Mine hurt from *walking.*"

"Who cares if someone sees us flying?" William demanded. "Thanks to your daughter, every farmer in Ash Grove already knows we have come back."

Alida bit her lip.

"Why not let us fly up to bed at night and down in the morning?" Kary's mother said. "Or let us make faerie lights at least. Someone is going to fall and get hurt in the dark."

"Maybe we should just give up trying to live here and go back into hiding!" William said.

Everyone hushed at the anger in his voice.

"Is that what you want to do? Leave our home again?"

Alida blinked, astonished. It was her father, and he was shouting. He looked more upset than she had ever seen him.

No one answered.

No one spoke at all for a long moment. Then her mother did, quietly and kindly.

"When we left this meadow, long ago, many of you argued with me and wanted to stay. While we were living in the other place, many of you kept complaining. Now we are back where we belong.

You may do what you wish. I intend to stay here."

Alida blinked. Would some of the faeries decide to leave on their own? She waited for someone to answer her mother, but no one did.

Her father stared at William, then at the others, one by one. When he finally spoke, he wasn't shouting anymore.

"If Lord Dunraven doesn't find out about us, it will be because the humans in Ash Grove are grateful to our daughter." He shook his head. "We all just *hoped* they wouldn't starve. She made sure they wouldn't."

Alida felt her heart lift.

No matter what anyone else thought, her family was proud of her.

The argument went on, but Alida didn't stay to listen. Instead she walked the woods until she had found four more good logs. Then three more after that.

On the way home each time, she practiced

making the logs stand upright. It was very hard to hold them steady, and it kept her from thinking about Ellen, what William had said, and everything else. By the time she went to supper, no one was arguing—they were barely talking.

High in her faerie's nest that night, Alida lay awake, staring at the rising moon while her sister slept.

Her mother kept saying they had to be patient.

But if they kept hiding, nothing would ever change. How would the villagers ever learn to trust faeries if they never even saw any? Ten years from now the faeries would still be hiding, hoping that Lord Dunraven's guards wouldn't come.

Alida sat up, careful not to wake Terra.

She needed to talk to Gavin.

He was human.

He could help her figure out what to do.

She slid from beneath her blanket and perched on the edge of the nest. Terra was breathing soft and slow.

Alida tucked her shawl beneath her arm, spread her wings, and glided silently to the ground. She ran all the way to the far end of the clearing before she flew upward to perch in a pine tree. Then she held still, breathless, listening.

There was no sound. No one was awake, no one had heard the whirring of her wings.

She jumped back into the air.

She flew high and swift over the treetops.

It took a little time for her to spot the road that went past Ruth Oakes's house.

Once she did, she flew lower, following it.

Just seeing the neat cottage and the flower garden behind it made her smile.

She perched in a tall tree until she spotted Kip, Ruth's dog. He was curled up on the back porch, so she went around to the front.

Careful not to make a sound, Alida peeked into the windows until she saw Gavin. He was asleep. She tapped lightly on the glass. He woke up.

Alida lifted her head to make sure he could see her in the moonlight. He smiled, but then she saw worry in his eyes.

The window creaked as he opened it.

"Nothing is wrong," she whispered. "I just need your advice."

"Do you want to come in?" he whispered back.

She shook her head.

Gavin nodded and pulled his curtain closed just long enough to get dressed. Then he swung one leg over the windowsill. Together they walked back up on the road.

Alida listened to the sound of the road grit beneath his shoes. Her own bare feet made no sound at all.

It was odd, how noisy humans were compared to faeries.

"I miss you," she said, once they were far enough away from the house.

He smiled. "I think about you, too. And I wonder

what your aunt Lily and William are arguing about."

Alida laughed before she could stop herself, then clapped one hand over her mouth.

Gavin held very still. They were both silent, listening. But there was no sound from the direction of the house. No one had heard her. Not even Kip.

"I've heard you fly past three or four times," he said. "Or maybe it was the wind and I was just wishing it was you."

She smiled, then looked at the ground. "It was the wind. My mother asked me not to come."

"I'm glad you did," he said. "Lord Dunraven was here today—with his daughter and a few guards." When Alida didn't look surprised, he arched his eyebrows. "Did you know?"

Alida told him what had happened.

Gavin sighed. "Ruth tried to help his daughter and couldn't. They had to use a wagon to get her back to the castle."

Alida looked at the stars. "It was my fault."

"There are fallen limbs all over the woods, Alida," Gavin said. "No one should gallop headlong like that on a path they don't know well."

Alida nodded.

It was true.

But it didn't make her feel better. If she hadn't panicked, Ellen would not have gotten hurt.

"Do you think anyone from Ash Grove has told Lord Dunraven we're here?" she asked.

He shook his head. "And Ruth says by midwinter—when they would have been starving— even the ones who want to hate faeries will have to admit you saved them. She intends to talk to them at Winter Feast."

"I wish we could come too," Alida said.

Gavin smiled. "That's a good idea. They'd find out you aren't much different from us."

Alida sighed. "But what if Lord Dunraven and his guards happened to come?"

"The Dunravens visit relatives for Winter Feast,"

Gavin told her. "Most of the guards stay at the castle—they almost never ride during the worst of the winter."

"Would the humans really want us to come?" she asked Gavin.

He hesitated, then shook his head. "Not all of them, but I'll ask Ruth about it. She's been their healer for a long time. If anyone can talk them into it, she can."

Flying home, threading her way through the trees, Alida was full of hope.

Maybe everything would work out. Maybe the faeries and the Ash Grove farmers could be friends after all.

She decided not to tell anyone.

She didn't want to admit she had gone to see Gavin after her mother asked her not to.

But it was more than that.

What if the villagers *didn't* invite them?

Chapter

6

The next day was blustery and cold.

So was the one after that.

The wind made the pine trees shudder, and it loosened the last of the brown leaves from the oaks and scattered them over the ground.

Alida stayed busy.

Almost every day she added to the growing pile of heavy, straight logs to strengthen the walls of the shelter.

And every day she got better at using the lifting magic. When she made mistakes, she just jumped back and let the logs crash to the ground. Then she would start over.

Once she had gotten really good at it, she started making up games.

At first she held the massive logs straight up and down. Then she practiced making them bob up and down, like they were hopping down the road. Sometimes she made them zigzag, barely missing one another. Terra saw her one day and was amazed. "Aldous and his parents can't do that."

Alida smiled. It was fun. And when she was busy, she had less time to worry.

Sometimes, if it was too cold, she worked in the weavers' house, or washed milk curds for the cheese makers. She saw her parents often, but they were both so busy she barely talked to them.

She barely talked to anyone. Every evening she hoped the next day would bring people from Ash Grove to invite the faeries to their Winter Feast.

She wanted to stop hiding her friendship with Gavin. She wanted all the faeries to have human friends. And she knew she should have brought

Ellen to the meadow. If anyone could figure out how to mend human bones, it was her mother. She was furious with herself for being so afraid.

But how could she have risked it?

Every time she thought about what had happened to Ellen, it made her sad.

Lord Dunraven's cruel and terrible law hurt everyone.

Even his own daughter.

Alida's father and the men working with him finally finished digging the shelter.

They began smoothing out the floor.

They used magic to roll the heaviest, straightest log back and forth, slowly, over and over. Alida watched when she could. The dirt got harder and harder.

A few days later, her father told her they were about to begin using the logs she and Terra and others had worked so hard to find.

Alida got up early.

She climbed a pine tree close to the pit and watched.

It was clear that all the men had become very good at using lifting magic to dig—but they hadn't ever tried moving heavy logs.

While she was watching, they let the logs fall back to the ground and began to argue.

Alida climbed down and spent the rest of the day separating thistledown—and thinking.

That evening she watched for her father and ran to walk beside him. "Could I help build the shelter?" she asked. "I've gotten good at balancing logs."

He stopped and looked at her. "I saw you watching us. Can you do better than that?"

She nodded. "Much better. I've been practicing a lot."

"I'll let you try," he said. "But if you can't, I'll ask you to leave. We have to finish the walls so we can build the roof before it snows hard."

The next morning, just before sunrise, her father woke her.

She followed him across the meadow, through the tangle of bushes, past the cheese makers' and weavers' houses.

He stopped at the edge of the pit and pointed at a ladder. "It would be easier to fly, but your mother insisted."

Alida climbed down.

"Take a look around," her father called to her. "I'll be back."

Alida nodded, without looking up at him. The pit seemed even bigger once she was standing inside it.

It was so deep that she couldn't see anything but the sky when she looked up.

Walking along the wall, she noticed a deep trench that went all the way around.

She paced the length of the shelter, then the width, counting her steps.

The shelter was fifty steps wide and sixty steps long. There would be room for everyone if they needed shelter from a snowstorm—or anything else. She suddenly wondered how many grass mats they would have to weave to cover the floor.

Alida looked at the trench again. It was deep and wide. That had to be where her father would want to set the logs.

Waiting for him to come back, she noticed a shadow on the far wall and went to look.

It wasn't a shadow. It was the opening of a tunnel.

She started looking and found two more.

All of them were wide and low, just big enough for faeries to fly through. Humans were much taller. They would have to bend over, or crawl.

She followed one of the tunnels for a little ways, then turned back. As she came out into the sunlight, she saw her father on the ladder.

She ran to hug him.

"This is wonderful. It's amazing. Does Mother know about the—"

"Tunnels?" he interrupted. "Yes. It was her idea.

They run in different directions. The longest one goes most of the way to Ash Grove. And there is magic to make them impossible to see and—"

"Good morning!" someone shouted. There were four men starting down the ladder. Their billowing cloaks hid their wings.

"You know my daughter Alida," her father said, once the men were standing in a loose circle inside the unroofed shelter.

Two of them smiled—Trina's father Thomas, and a man named Porter. The others just nodded. Alida tried to smile back, but she was nervous.

"Alida has been gathering logs for us for a long time," her father was saying. "She wants to help us put them in place."

He looked at her. "Ready?"

The men glanced at one another, and Alida could tell they didn't think she could do it.

She took a deep breath. "I should set them down into the trench?"

"Yes," her father said. "Upright, as close together as possible. We'll pack dirt around them and then use the new binding magic."

Alida climbed up the ladder and looked through the pile of logs. She chose a wide, heavy one.

She concentrated hard as she made the magic. Then she lifted the log very carefully. She walked to the edge of the huge pit and lowered it slowly to the hard-packed earth.

She chose two more logs and laid them beside it. Then she went down the ladder again.

Her father used his cutting magic to make all the logs the right height.

Then he stepped back.

The men had all moved to one side to watch.

Alida lifted the biggest of the three logs first.

"Start at a corner," her father said.

Alida nodded and pushed the log through the air. She set it into the trench by the wall, tilted it back and forth until it was straight, then held it in place and divided the magic to pick up the second log.

She set it in the trench, then made it hop up and down, moving it a little closer to the first log with every hop.

She slid the third log through the air and slammed it into the first two to push them even closer together. Then she set it in the trench.

None of the men made a sound until she had the heavy log in place.

Then they all started talking at once. They wanted her to teach them, and they welcomed her help. Alida blushed and smiled, feeling wonderful. She spent that morning explaining how she had worked the lifting magic.

Three of the men—including her father—learned enough to start placing the logs.

The others moved dampened earth back into the trench once the logs were in place. By late afternoon, one whole wall was finished.

They were all tired, but the logs were straight

and true. Where they didn't touch, Alida could see the dirt wall behind them.

"I have been practicing the binding magic," her father said. "Trying to make it strong enough."

He turned, and Alida heard him whispering a few of the ancient words her mother had taught her—and some she didn't recognize.

Suddenly there were no gaps at all. Alida walked closer and ran her hand over the wood.

The binding magic was amazing.

The logs hadn't moved.

They had *grown together*. The dirt wall behind them was sealed off, completely covered in wood.

Trina's father smiled. "I'm glad we have two such worthy princesses. We all know Terra is happy as a musician and one of our very best. It's good to know my children will also have Alida's cleverness to lead them."

Alida felt herself blush.

She walked to supper with her father, feeling odd.

She couldn't imagine making all the decisions her mother had to make. It still scared her. But maybe it was like practicing magic. Maybe she could learn how.

At supper, Trina's father described what Alida had done. The faeries cheered. Then he explained her father's new magic, and they cheered again.

Alida went to bed tired and happy.

The next day they finished two walls. Five days after that, the work was done. Her father stood up during supper and told everyone to come see the shelter first thing in the morning.

Alida got up early. It was fun to watch the faeries' faces.

They were as amazed as she had been.

Everyone spoke quietly, running their hands across the solid, tree-bark walls.

They peered into the tunnels. Some of the little faeries ran in circles, chasing one another across the huge pit. Alida loved knowing she had helped make the shelter. Now all it needed was a roof.

Chapter

7

After three days the clouds cleared.

A bright autumn sun warmed the meadow a little. Everyone was busy doing all kinds of chores. Some of the faeries helped the cheese makers enlarge the root cellar so they could store all the cheeses they had made. The weavers worked day and night to make grass mats and covered the floor of the shelter. One of the cows had a late calf, and three of the older fairies built an extra shed for the mother and baby.

Alida's father showed her the new binding magic. It was difficult.

She practiced it constantly, and she did it in the

woods so no one would see her. Most of the faeries were getting used to the idea of new magic—but some were still uneasy about it.

On the fourth day, Alida's father explained how they would make the roof. "We need vines to bind together for the roof—strong, dry vines that have died back for winter," he said. "Berries, ivy, wild grapes . . ."

The faeries began talking all at once. Alida's mother quieted them and made sure they all understood how to stack the vines. Three days later, on a cold, windy morning, her father looked at the huge piles and told everyone he thought they had enough.

Five faeries, including Alida's mother, lifted the vines into the air.

The weavers used their magic to tangle them together.

Then Alida and her father used the new magic.

Alida watched, amazed, as the vines grew

together like the logs had. The roof would be as solid and strong as the walls of the shelter.

Everyone helped finish the shelter. They used simple lifting magic to cover the roof with the dirt that had been piled all around the huge pit. Then they scattered leaves, twigs, and acorns over the dirt. When they were finished, the shelter was invisible; it looked like a little hill that had always been part of the forest.

Alida could not stop smiling. It was amazing. The shelter had two doors and three tunnels. The doors didn't *look* like doors. No human would ever spot them. The entrances to the tunnels were hidden the same way, with bushes and trees—and magic.

A few days later, some of the men built sheds for the cows and goats, using small logs and no magic at all.

Wooden pegs held everything together.

Then they added pegs to the weavers' and cheese makers' houses so they didn't look magical, even though they were.

Alida's mother waited until supper to explain to all the faeries at once. "If human travelers or Dunraven's guards ever search the meadow, even if they find our buildings, they still won't know anything here is faerie-made. And while they are trying to find out who lives here, we will hide in the shelter. We can use the tunnels to escape if we must."

There was a silence, then everyone cheered. They shouted loud and long, and Alida's mother didn't hush them.

Alida felt a weight leave her heart. They were safer than they had ever been.

Everyone was relieved. As the days passed, there were fewer arguments.

The weather turned cold, but the men went on working, *inside* the shelter. Some men built cabinets to hold everyone's clothing and the new blankets the weavers had made.

One bitter cold day the faeries carried their

wooden supper tables inside and began eating in the shelter too.

The elders were the first to sleep inside instead of their treetop nests—including William. Then the families with little children did too.

Inside the shelter everyone could make faerie lights and noise, without being afraid. Terra and the other musicians began to practice again. The thick shelter walls kept the sound inside.

It snowed hard one day, then again the next as winter settled in. "Maybe we could have a Winter Feast," Aunt Lily said one evening. "We have twenty days or so before the full moon."

Alida lowered her head so that no one would see how disappointed she was that the humans hadn't invited the faeries to come to Ash Grove, and as much as Gavin had liked the idea, they probably weren't going to.

Not yet.

Maybe next year.

"How can we have a Winter Feast *indoors*?" William asked loudly. "Faeries watch the full moon rise at Winter Feast. They don't burrow underground like squirrels!"

Alida smiled when four or five faeries started to argue with him, then with one another.

It took five days of talking to settle the question.

They would all go outside together to watch the full moon rise. Then they would celebrate inside the shelter, where it would be safe to have music and the loud laughter of children playing games.

Preparations began.

Alida's mother still asked young faeries to take turns keeping watch, but everyone else worked on getting ready for Winter Feast.

The musicians practiced every day, inside the shelter.

Terra had composed a beautiful new song. Aldous listened to her practice whenever he could.

The cheese makers worked in their usual house

all day, rolling a batch of special salted curds in herbs and pepperbark.

Alida's mother insisted on using their fancy dishes and tables, so the weavers began making bright cloths to cover them.

Every day the faeries were less afraid. For the first time in her life, Alida began to understand how things had been before old Lord Dunraven had made his terrible law.

Chapter

8

Late one afternoon, Alida and her mother were outside the cheese house when the sound of whirring wings made them both turn.

The two young faeries who had been on watch came swooping into the meadow. They flew over the uneven circle of bushes and trees and dropped to the ground in front of Alida and her mother.

"We heard voices!" the taller boy whispered. "Human voices!"

Alida's mother nodded and bent close to whisper in Alida's ear. "Please go see who it is. Be very careful to stay hidden and come back quickly. I'll make sure everyone gets into the shelter."

Alida took a quick breath. "Which direction?" she asked the boy.

He pointed.

Alida nodded, took off her shawl and tied it around her waist, then leapt into the air. She flew high and swift, listening hard.

Had Dunraven's guards finally come?

Once she was close enough to hear the voices, her heart lifted.

It wasn't guards.

It was Ruth Oakes and people from Ash Grove! They were all talking, laughing.

Alida found a tree perch high above them.

She spotted Gavin and his grandmother, Molly. She recognized some of the others from the night they had caught her when she came back to make their crops reappear. All the humans were wearing thick, long coats, and their cheeks were rosy from the cold.

Alida was so excited—were they just here to

visit, or to invite the faeries to their Winter Feast? She almost flew down to greet them. Then she remembered that the rest of the faeries were in the shelter.

She waited until a breeze stirred the trees, then flew straight upward, so the villagers wouldn't hear her wings.

Flying low, she skimmed the tops of the trees and landed inside the circle of bushes. She sprinted to the shelter door and ran to tell everyone the good news.

"Are you sure there are no guards with them?" William asked.

"I'm sure," Alida said. Then she started for the entrance, hoping everyone would follow her. Some of the faeries stood up.

"Wait," her mother said. "It will look odd if we all come walking out of the bushes at once."

Alida stopped. Her mother was right. As much as she trusted Gavin, his grandmother, and Ruth

Oakes, it was foolish to make the other humans notice the circle of bushes and berries.

"We could fly down the tunnel that leads to the egg-shaped rock," she said. "Then we can all cover our wings and walk back up to greet the humans."

Alida's mother nodded. "Yes! Hurry!"

One by one the faeries flew. Parents carried their children.

Alida joined the line.

The tunnel wasn't too long, and once she came out into the daylight again, she ran to catch up with the faeries who were ahead of her.

It was perfect.

They all looked like they were walking home from the woods beyond the meadow. The humans would stand twenty steps from everything the faeries had built—and never know it.

Gavin hugged Alida, then Aunt Lily and almost everyone else.

They were all so glad to see him.

Ruth and Molly were smiling. The others stood back a little ways.

Alida watched their eyes flicker from one faerie to the next, then the next.

Maybe most of the humans hadn't realized how many of them there were?

Alida saw Mr. Dawer. He waved when he noticed her looking at him. She waved back. He had listened to Gavin the night the farmers had been so angry— and he had given her a chance to prove she had come to help them. The farm girl who had thought she was a thief was there too.

Alida smiled at her.

She smiled back.

"We want to invite you to our Winter Feast," Ruth said once everyone quieted.

Alida glanced at the elders.

They all looked stunned.

Alida's mother turned. "Our neighbors have

invited us to Winter Feast!" she said, then arched her eyebrows in a silent question.

Alida nodded, then Terra and her father did, then, one by one, so did the others.

Even William.

Even Lily.

Alida's mother turned back to Ruth. "Thank you for the invitation. We have honey to spare and berry jam. And our musicians have been practicing. They could play."

"Wonderful!" Ruth said. "Please come to my house at noon on the day of the full moon. We can all walk to the town hall together."

Alida heard murmurs behind her. Everyone was nodding, smiling.

She turned. Gavin was busy introducing his grandmother to everyone. The farm girl was staring at the faeries. All the humans were.

By the time they left, Alida was so happy she

could barely speak. Maybe the rest of the faeries would make human friends.

If they did, they would learn what she had learned. Some human beings were wonderful.

Maybe the faeries would understand why Gavin was like a brother to her. Maybe she could see him more often.

The very next day, the faeries began to plan. Alida's mother asked her to come to the weavers' house—and Alida was afraid she was going to end up helping to separate thistledown again. But her mother had a surprise for her.

The weavers had made her a beautiful dress the color of dark roses.

She tried it on.

The cloth was so light that it almost floated in the air.

It made her feel beautiful. "It was for our Winter Feast," her mother said. "But it will do for the humans' celebration too, I think."

That night, after supper, the faeries agreed that they should wear shoes and hide their wings at the feast, to help the humans think of everything they shared with faeries—not their differences.

"We should take a few of our new blankets for their elders," Kary said.

Alida was surprised when her mother disagreed. "They aren't like anything the humans weave. What if they show them to friends from another village? We still have to be careful."

Alida knew her mother was right, and it made her sad.

Two days before Winter Feast, it began to snow.

By the time everyone was dressed up and ready to fly to Ruth's house, the snow was knee deep.

The young faeries were all giggling and fidgeting.

The musicians had left their harps in the shelter, but they were all carrying their flutes. Some of the men held bags of jars filled with honey and jam.

Alida's mother sent two swift fliers to make sure there were no strangers in the woods.

Once they came back, she asked everyone to form a long, loose line.

"Keep track of your children," she called out. "Remember we have to cross the road at least once, so be ready to stop and hide if we need to."

The faeries pulled off their shawls and cloaks and tied them around their waists. When everyone was ready, Alida's mother opened her wings and leapt upward. They all followed, flying low through the trees.

They were close to the road when the line suddenly slowed.

Alida couldn't see, but she heard hoofbeats.

Her mother flew back down the line, gesturing for them all to perch in the pine trees and wait. Alida found a place to hide and held her breath.

They all did.

Except for the sound of the horses, the forest was silent.

When the humans appeared around a bend in the road, Alida could see three guards on dun-colored horses. Then came one of Lord Dunraven's fancy, painted carriages. The harnessed horses were blowing out long, steamy breaths.

Alida saw the humans in the carriage for only an instant as it passed, but she recognized Lord Dunraven and the pale girl beside him.

It was Ellen.

She was bundled up in a woolen coat, leaning against her father's shoulder.

Chapter

9

The faeries waited for the sound of the horses' hooves to fade to silence.

Then they crossed.

Once they were back in the woods, they flew faster than any horse could ever gallop, taking a straight line toward Ruth Oakes's house.

Ruth came out to greet them. "My little cottage will never hold all of you," she apologized. "But my dog is locked inside the barn, so you are welcome to walk around, or there's a fire in the hearth if anyone needs to warm themselves for a few minutes."

Some of the elders went inside to get warm. So did some of the mothers with babies.

Alida hugged Gavin, Ruth, and Molly, then listened as her mother described what they had seen on the road.

Ruth looked puzzled. "Lord Dunraven has two cousins among the other lords, and he visits them for Winter Feast—but he has always gone five or six days before the full moon."

"How long will it take them to get this far?" Alida's mother asked.

Ruth shrugged. "With the snow? It'll be early evening before they pass my house—if they don't turn back long before that." She gestured at the cloudy sky. It was dark gray at the horizon.

Alida faced the wind. "Maybe they already have."

"Let's walk the river path instead of the road," Molly said. "Just to be safe."

Ruth led them down the narrow lane. They passed a broken-down little house that looked empty. Beyond that was the river. Then the path ran through tall, withered grass.

Gavin walked beside Alida. "We held a town meeting to decide if they would ask you to come," he whispered.

Alida looked up at him. "Did they argue?"

Gavin nodded. "But not for long. They hate old Lord Dunraven's law too."

A gust of cold wind rushed across the field.

The humans and the faeries all lowered their heads and hunched their shoulders. Then they all began to walk faster.

When the faeries followed Ruth off the path and into town, Alida heard them whispering. Many of them had been in Ash Grove before, just not for a long, long time.

The houses and shops were made of wood planks or bricks. The streets were narrow. Alida saw human children staring at them through a window.

"Listen!" Gavin said as they turned a corner.

Over the wind, Alida heard voices: People were singing.

When they turned the last corner, she caught her breath.

The town hall was bigger than any of the other buildings—and there were lanterns in all the windows.

At nightfall it would be beautiful.

Just as the song ended, Ruth pulled open the big doors. "Our neighbors have arrived," she announced. All the humans turned to face them.

"This is the child who helped us save our harvest," she said, and put her arm around Alida's shoulders.

Alida felt her heart thudding. There were a hundred or more humans in the huge room, and every one of them was looking at her.

Some of them were whispering to one another as Ruth waited for all the faeries to come inside.

She gestured at the tables full of food and sweets. The faeries added what they had brought.

"Please don't let us interrupt your music," Alida's father said after a moment. "It was lovely."

The singers began a soft, slow song. Some of the humans began to dance. Alida's parents joined them. They danced carefully, making sure they didn't bump into anyone.

When the song ended and another one began, her mother and father stood still as the music got louder and faster. Then Alida saw her mother look at her father, her eyebrows arched. He nodded.

She took off her shawl.

He set his cape aside.

For a moment everyone stopped talking and stared at them—at their wings.

Alida stood off to one side. She watched the humans' faces light up when her father lifted her mother and turned in a circle.

When he did it a second time, a few of them clapped their hands. Alida was startled, but Gavin leaned close and told her that clapping was like cheering.

The lively music went on. Some of the other faeries found partners and joined in.

Some uncovered their wings.

Some didn't.

After a while, the humans stopped staring.

When Terra asked Gavin if he wanted to dance, Alida saw people—and faeries—watching them.

Gavin was terrible, and Terra tried to teach him. They were both laughing.

Then she danced with Aldous. They were so good at all the difficult steps that *everyone* stopped to watch.

After a while, the faerie musicians got out their flutes and began to play.

Alida saw one man and his wife practicing a twirling step her mother and father had done. After three or four songs, they were doing it perfectly.

Ruth Oakes caught her eye and winked.

Alida smiled. This was working out better than she had ever thought it could.

Someone tapped her shoulder.

It startled her, and she spun around.

Old William was standing behind her. "Dancing

is easy," he told her. "Watch. Do what I do." He took two steps to his right, then one to his left. Alida was blushing, but she copied him.

He showed her how to twirl around without losing her balance. By the end of the song, she was having fun.

When the music stopped, he kissed her hands, then tapped Aunt Lily's shoulder. They danced to the next song.

When the musicians stopped long enough to eat, they could all hear the wind rattling the roof shingles.

It got worse.

One human family decided to go home. Then three more families put on their coats. The icy wind roared into the hall every time someone opened the door to leave.

"We can't thank you enough for inviting us," Alida's mother said over the sound of the wind. "But I think we should go now too."

A sudden gust of wind pounded the building.

When Gavin hugged her good-bye, Alida stood on her tiptoes. "What's the road like beyond Ruth's house?" she whispered.

He leaned close so she could hear him over the wind. "It's steep and rutted all the way along the ridge, and worse after that."

Alida retied her shawl and followed the others outside. Her mother walked along the line, making sure the families were ready. "Help Trina's sister with her children if she needs it," she said when she went by.

Alida nodded. "Gavin says the road is bad past Ruth's house, so Lord Dunraven might be turning back."

Her mother kissed her cheek. "We'll be careful."

Once they were outside, the wind shoved at them. It was strong and gusty, far too dangerous to fly in. Alida thought her mother might lead them right back into the town hall.

But she set off walking.

Alida found Trina's sister and offered to carry her toddler as they walked through the snowy fields. She snuggled the little girl against her chest as they crossed the road and veered into the woods. The wind got stronger.

It was bending the trees as Alida's father went up and down the line, explaining: They were not walking all the way home. They were going to use one of the new tunnels.

When they finally got close to the hidden entrance, Alida's mother made a tiny faerie light and held it out as she walked forward.

When the magical light shone on a thick clump of blueberry bushes, they disappeared.

Suddenly the opening of the tunnel was easy to see.

Alida saw the faeries glancing at one another, smiling as they all followed her mother inside.

"The entrance closes itself," her mother called. "Make faerie lights so we can fly."

Lights appeared in the darkness. The sound of the wind faded.

Alida's mother stretched her wings and flew, following the gentle curve of the silent tunnel. The only sound was the whirr of their wings and a few tired babies fussing.

The shelter was even quieter. Was the storm still battering the woods? It was impossible to tell. Trina's sister thanked Alida and took her little daughter back.

Everyone was tired.

The faeries who hadn't been sleeping inside were getting blankets out of the new cabinets to make nests on the soft grass mats. No one wanted to be outside tonight. Not even William.

Alida lay awake in the near silence for a long time. She could not stop thinking about Ellen Dunraven, hoping her father had turned back early, that they were at least halfway home—and that the storm was easing.

Careful not to make a sound, Alida finally got up and put on her shawl.

She tiptoed back down the tunnel.

When she was sure that no one would see it, she made a faerie light, took off her shawl, and flew as fast as she could.

Chapter
10

When Alida came out of the tunnel and into the dark forest, the wind had eased a little and she even caught a glimpse of the full moon. The clouds were breaking up.

She memorized the shapes of the trees near the tunnel entrance.

When she was sure she could find her way back, she flew toward Ash Grove.

The lanterns in the town hall had all been put out.

There was only one still lit in Ruth's house.

As the moon came out, Alida flew faster.

If the Dunravens had turned back, she would see nothing but empty road.

If they hadn't, she should be able to catch up now that the wind had calmed.

The instant she spotted the carriage horses trotting through the snow, she would turn around and go home.

Alida flew high and fast, so she could see long stretches of the empty road all at once. Gavin had been right: The road was steep and rutted.

Coming around a long curve, she saw something in the distance. She slowed and flew lower as she got close. It was just a fallen tree, half buried in the snow.

The next part of the road snaked back and forth up the steep ridge.

At the top, Alida saw another dark shape in the moonlight.

She flew faster. It was the coach. For an instant she was relieved and happy.

Then she realized it wasn't moving.

The horses weren't trotting along. They were standing still. And there was no sign of the guards.

Alida swooped closer. The coach was tipped sideways, one wheel in a deep rut. The horses were still hitched to it, cold, miserable, their heads low. They were standing as close together as they could.

Alida perched high in a pine and stared.

Where were the guards? Why hadn't they unhitched the carriage horses for Lord Dunraven and Ellen to ride?

The moonlight dimmed.

Alida looked up. More clouds were coming in. Maybe the storm wasn't over.

She jumped off her perch and glided down to land at the edge of the trees.

She listened for hoofbeats, then tied her shawl over her wings before she walked out onto the dark road.

The horses were glad to see her, and they weren't

hurt, but the wheel was wedged into the rut. Alida wasn't sure what to do. She could unhitch the horses and lead them back to Ruth's house. But if there were guards on the road, they would think she had stolen them and—

Alida heard something squeak.

She tensed, ready to fly.

Then the sound came again. Breathless, Alida made a tiny faerie light and held it out, bending to peer through the round little window in the coach door.

Ellen and her father were both inside. He was asleep, wrapped up in an embroidered blanket.

Ellen's eyes were wide open.

Alida ducked backward and put out her faerie light.

She heard the window slide open.

"Hello?" Ellen whispered. "Is someone there?"

Wind swirled across the road, and clumps of snow fell from pine branches behind Alida. She whirled around—it had sounded like hoofbeats.

"Please don't leave," Ellen whispered. "Please. We need help."

"Where are the guards?" Alida asked her.

"I don't know," Ellen said, and her voice trembled. "My father tried to walk to Ash Grove for help, but the wind was terrible and he turned back. He is so cold. Please don't leave us here. Please."

Alida stepped back in the darkness and pulled off her shawl. She pushed it through the slit in the window. "Put this on."

"I'll make sure my father doesn't blame you for anything, no matter what happens," Ellen whispered. "I give you my word. Please, just help us."

"I won't leave," Alida promised, remembering Ellen's first promise to her. It had to be terrible to have a father everyone feared.

Staying away from the little window, Alida made a tiny faerie light and looked beneath the carriage again. "The wheel is broken," she told the shivering horses. "I need your help."

One of the horses reached out to smell her hair. The other one shook the snow off its back and pawed at the ground. Alida rubbed their ears and sang a little faerie song to them.

Then she used lifting magic to raise the coach, gently, slowly, until she could see all four of the wooden wheels a hand's span off the ground.

Then, letting the horses make most of the decisions, she led them down the hill, holding the coach level and steady with magic.

It was a long and dangerous walk, and Alida was starting to shiver a little when she finally got to Ruth's house.

She led the horses to the porch, then ran to the door and knocked hard.

When it swung open, Alida inhaled the familiar scents of herbs and healing teas.

Ruth was in her nightgown.

"Alida, is everything—" she began, then saw the coach.

"Lord Dunraven and his daughter got stranded," Alida told her. "They are both cold and exhausted and—"

"Wake Gavin!" Ruth said. "He can help me carry—"

"I can do it," Alida said. She ran to the coach and flung open the door.

Lord Dunraven was closest—motionless, asleep. She gathered her magic quickly and lifted him first.

Ruth ran inside and laid three soft, thick blankets beside the hearth, then watched Alida guide the sleeping Lord Dunraven through the air. When Alida laid him down, he made a low, unhappy sound, but he didn't open his eyes. In the firelight, Alida could see how pale he was.

She ran back outside and lifted Ellen out of the coach.

Gavin and his grandmother were awake when she came back in. They stood still, watching Ellen Dunraven float past them.

Gavin gestured down the hall. "Ruth said you should put her in my bed," he whispered. "I'll get the horses into the barn. You should cover your wings."

Feeling foolish, Alida settled Ellen onto the still warm bed, then gently untangled her shawl and pulled it free. Once she had it on, she slid Ellen's shoes off. They didn't match. The right shoe had been specially made to fit the twisted shape of her foot. Alida stared at it, then tucked the blankets around her.

Alida was close to tears when she went into the kitchen.

Molly made her sit down and drink a cup of rosemary and peachskin tea.

When it was half gone, Gavin came in.

He went straight to the cookstove and warmed his hands. "The horses are all right, I think. Just cold and hungry."

Alida didn't answer him. She couldn't stop thinking about Ellen, about that day in the woods.

Ruth came in and sat down. She smiled a thin, tight smile. "Dunraven must be recovering. He said he'd send guards to arrest me if I harmed him or his daughter in any way. Then he went back to sleep."

Everyone smiled a little, except Alida.

"I probably shouldn't have brought them here," she said. "I just couldn't think of anywhere else and—" She wiped her eyes, then looked at Ruth. "It's my fault that Ellen got hurt. Isn't there some way to heal her?"

Ruth touched Alida's cheek in a way that reminded her of her mother. "I couldn't do it alone. But perhaps together we can. Let's go see."

Alida followed her down the hall.

Without waking Ellen, Ruth looked at her twisted ankle. She touched the odd bump, then gently flexed Ellen's foot.

Ellen stirred, and they lowered the blanket and stepped back into the hallway.

Alida looked at Ruth. "Can we fix it?"

Ruth led her to the kitchen. She broke off three twigs of dried rosemary and arranged them on the table. "This is how the bones should be. But they're like this," she said. She broke one twig almost in half, and lay it across the other two.

Alida stared at the twigs, then rearranged them. "So if I could bind this one back together, then move it into its proper place, do you think it would heal?"

Ruth nodded slowly. "It might. The way it is now, it never will."

Alida sat still. This was her fault. But if things went wrong, Lord Dunraven would be furious at Ruth and Molly and Gavin and all the faeries, not just her. But if she didn't try, Ellen was doomed to live in her locked room, forever in pain, unable to ride, to walk. . . .

Alida looked up at Ruth. "I have to try. "

Ruth nodded. "I will help any way I can."

Chapter

11

A lida borrowed a candle lantern, excused herself, and went down the hall.

She slid the blanket back carefully and looked at Ellen's foot again.

She imagined what she would do, how she would guide the magic, splitting it in half to hold the two smaller bones straight while she moved the broken one.

Then Alida took a deep breath and touched Ellen's shoulder.

She sat up, rubbing her eyes. "Where is my father?"

"Just down the hall, sleeping peacefully," Alida

said. She held the candle lantern higher, so that Ellen could see her face.

Ellen narrowed her eyes, then smiled. "I remember you! Is this your house? Thank your parents for me and—"

"I need to tell you something," Alida interrupted her. "It's my fault that you got hurt. I can explain later. But I think I can heal your ankle."

Ellen stared at her. "My father's physicians said there was nothing they could do. That's why we were traveling. My father heard about another healer in Bindenfast. He uses heat and tight bandages, which can hurt terribly, but—"

"But he won't be able to use magic," Alida said.

Ellen caught her breath and stared.

"Yes," Alida said, before she could ask. "I am a faerie."

Ellen's voice softened and she looked down, then back at Alida. "I want to ride again. I want to walk. I want to *run*."

"Promise me you will never tell anyone," Alida said.

Ellen met her eyes. "I always wanted the faerie stories our stableman told me to be true. I give you my solemn promise."

Alida asked her to lie down. She carefully, gently pressed on Ellen's foot until she could feel the bones, then formed the magic inside herself. The split was easier than she thought it would be. Moving the splintered bone back into place was much harder.

It took four tries.

Ellen's lips were pressed shut and her eyes were closed in pain, but she didn't make a sound.

Alida finally managed to hold the bones in place. Then she formed the binding magic.

Carefully, gradually, she joined the shattered bone back together.

When she was finished, she looked up. Ellen had fainted.

* * * *

Alida slept curled up on the carpet next to the bed and woke up in the dark to find that someone had draped a blanket over her. Her wings were cramped and aching beneath her shawl. She sat up and saw Ellen looking out the window. "Are you all right?" she whispered.

Ellen turned. "It worked," she said quietly. She stood up and walked a few steps, then sat on the edge of the bed again.

Alida smiled, her heart lighter than it had been in a long time. "Please act as though you are lame awhile longer—"

"I will," Ellen interrupted her. "And then I will pretend to get better very slowly. My father will never suspect anything." She reached out to clasp Alida's hand. "I've been lying awake, remembering all the stories our stableman told me. There was a faerie princess who was brought to the castle, he said. To keep her safe, the faeries had to promise to move far away and never to talk to people again. Do you know that story?"

Alida felt her heart stop, then start again. She nodded.

"I will one day rule my father's lands," Ellen said. "He has made it clear to everyone that he would rather have his own daughter rule than one of his nephews. When I can, I will get rid of the law. Please tell your queen that I promise her that."

"My mother will be very happy," Alida said quietly.

Ellen smiled. "The story said the princess was very brave."

Alida blushed, then lifted her head. "So it will be up to us one day," she said. "You and me."

Ellen nodded. "It will."

"And you promise the law will be stricken?"

Ellen nodded. "I give you my word."

They clasped hands, then hugged and said good-bye.

On her way out, Alida woke Gavin long enough

to whisper a good-bye and thank him for being her best friend.

Tiptoeing past Lord Dunraven, she slipped out the front door.

Then she freed her wings and flew home by the last light of the full moon. She couldn't wait to tell her mother what had happened, and that one day, faeries and humans could be friends again.

Read where it all began in

Moonsilver,

Book 1 of The Unicorn's Promise,
a companion series to The Faeries' Promise.

Heart Avimir was tired.

Everyone else had gone home.

It would be dark soon.

The stiff wheat stubble had scraped her hands bloody. There were long scratches on her bare feet.

Heart smiled. Her sack was half full. The harvesters had hurried through the fields this year, missing more grain than usual.

Lord Dunraven wouldn't like the gleaners finding so much fallen grain. But the people of Ash Grove were happy. They would have more bread this winter.

Lord Dunraven didn't need their little bit of gleaned wheat.

He owned every wheat field, every barley field, every hillside.

He owned the forest on the other side of the Blue River. The bridge that crossed the Blue River and the road that led to Derrytown belonged to him, too. Lord Dunraven owned towns and villages.

He owned everything.

Old Simon cleared his throat and spat. "What's that?" he asked, pointing.

Heart faced the sunset. Something was moving at the far end of the field, near the edge of a grove of old oak trees.

"A deer?" she replied.

"Looks like a cow," Simon said.

Heart squinted. "I can't tell." The animal was moving farther into the deep shadows.

"Whose cow would be out for wolves to find?" Simon asked. He tied up their wheat sacks with twine he kept in his pockets.

"I'll go see," Heart said.

Simon nodded. "Hurry back. No playing."

Heart glanced at Simon's angular face and thin gray hair. She wished that he loved her. But she knew he didn't.

Simon Pratt was not her father, after all. Nor was he an uncle or a grandfather or any kind of family.

Five years before, Simon had found her sleeping in the high grass by the Blue River. He had come upon her that morning the way someone stumbles across a nest of quail eggs.

Simon told her all about it. He'd been gathering firewood among the cottonwood trees by the river. She had been wrapped in a beautiful blanket, her hair knotted and tangled.

"Can you see what it is?" Simon shouted now.

Startled from her thoughts, Heart whirled around.

"Not yet!" she shouted over her shoulder. Whatever the animal was, it was deep in the dappled shade now.

Walking slowly toward the edge of the woods, Heart tried to recall something, anything, from before the morning Simon had awakened her in the tall grass.

She couldn't.

She never could.

Her first memory was this:

Her eyes had flown open and her breath had come quicker than a startled rabbit. And Simon had been there, leaning over her, with his sharpnosed face, his dark eyes and dark clothes.

And that was it.

Heart could remember everything back to that instant, perfectly. But then her memories just *ended*.

Simon had called her "Girl" for weeks. He had not named her. Ruth Oakes had done that. But he had fed her. She was alive. She knew she should be grateful.

But all the other children in Ash Grove knew their parents. They knew their grandparents and their great-grandparents. They didn't trust her. They wouldn't play with her, or even talk to her.

"What is it?" Simon called. "Why can't you see?"

Startled again, Heart stopped, peering into the dusky shade under the oak trees.

"It's a horse!" she called back, surprised. No one in Ash Grove owned horses, except Tin Blackaby. "A mare!"

"Then it's Blackaby's," Simon called. "Leave it alone!"

Heart nodded. She felt sorry for the horse.

Blackaby was Lord Dunraven's steward. He counted out crops and chicks and sheep and corn. He weighed out the peppers and onions people raised to sell to the Derrytown merchants. He told people how much they had to give to Lord Dunraven and how little they could keep. He was not kind. He worked his men and his horses hard.

"Blackaby's men will come," Simon shouted. "They'll think we're trying to steal it."

"Wait," Heart pleaded. "This isn't Tin Blackaby's horse."

"You're sure?" Simon shouted.

"Yes!" Heart called back. She could see the mare better now. It was white. She'd never seen a white horse in Tin Blackaby's corrals.

Coming close, Heart saw the mare's coat was rough, mud-speckled. She was thin, too, her ribs jutting out.

Her tail was full of river burrs.